ADVENTURE TIME™

WHICH WAY, DUDE?

#2

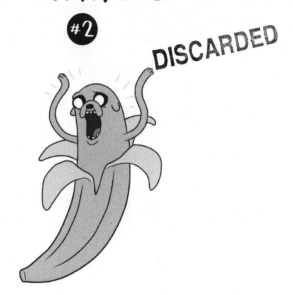

Jake Goes Bananas

WHICH WAY, DUDE?

Jake Goes Bananas

by Max Brallier
illustrated by Stephen Reed

PSS!
PRICE STERN SLOAN
An Imprint of Penguin Group (USA) LLC

PRICE STERN SLOAN
Published by the Penguin Group
Penguin Group (USA) LLC, 375 Hudson Street, New York, New York 10014, USA

USA | Canada | UK | Ireland | Australia | New Zealand | India | South Africa | China

penguin.com
A Penguin Random House Company

Published in 2013 by Price Stern Sloan, a division of Penguin Young Readers Group, 345 Hudson Street, New York, New York 10014. PSS! is a registered trademark of Penguin Group (USA) LLC. Printed in the U.S.A.

ISBN 978-0-8431-7526-4   10 9 8 7 6 5 4 3 2 1

LET'S GET THIS ADVENTURE STARTED!

Hey, gang!

It's us, *the dudes*—Finn and Jake! Welcome to our book. Today is *big*—it's Princess Bubblegum's b-day! And you know there ain't no party like a Candy Kingdom party.

But, of course, in the Land of Ooo, *nothing* ever goes as planned—and this party is about to get *started!*

Can you fix everything and save the day? We're about to find out, because this book is *not* like most books . . .

You'll be deciding how this adventure goes down! At the end of every chapter, you'll have a choice to make—sometimes you'll have to solve puzzles to help us out!

Along the way you'll earn **ADVENTURE MINUTES.** The more Adventure Minutes you earn, the more radical your journey! Whenever you earn Adventure Minutes, flip to page **121** so you can keep track of them. When you come to an ending, total up all your Adventure Minutes to figure out your total **ADVENTURE TIME!**

Good luck!

And remember . . . the future of the Candy Kingdom (and PB's party!) is in *your hands!*

BEGINNINGS
AND STUFF!

"Holy schmow! This party is serious business!" Finn exclaims.

Finn and Jake are walking through the Candy Kingdom. BMO waddles behind, and Marceline is all vamped out, floating next to them. Towering above the gang, in all its awesome glory, is the Candy Castle.

Today is Princess Bubblegum's Candy Carnival Birthday Bash, and the kingdom is *jumping*. The party is *ba-nay-nay*. In addition to the everyday Candy Kingdom fun, there are kick-butt games like Cookie-Karaoke, Peppermint-Pong, Sticky-Bunz Skee Ball, and Dunk the Doughnuts.

"Dude, I'm going to do *everything* at this birthday carnival," Jake says happily. "I will *own this carnival*!"

Princess Bubblegum is busy doing royal things like greeting visitors from other kingdoms, but she takes a moment to hop on over and greet her friends. "Hey!" Princess Bubblegum says. "What's up with you butts?"

"Happy birthday, PB! This is one serious shindig!" Jake says, eyeing her gifts. "Is that a giant chocolate-stuffed banana? Did someone get you a giant chocolate-stuffed banana? I want a chocolate-stuffed banana."

The princess smiles. "I already have, like, seventeen, so you can have this one, Jake."

Jake's face lights up "Really? You are one righteous princess, PB! And now, I'm going to go eat some fried butter and ride the Fudgy Ferris Wheel and Fruit-Loop-de-Loop until I barf."

But Jake's big party plans are interrupted—

There is a small *ding* noise, like a bell ringing, followed by a burst of light!

"What was that?" PB says, turning around.

Something flashes in the air. A door! A door is *unfolding* out of thin air. Finn knows what's going down . . .

"The Door Lord!" Finn exclaims. "I *hate* the Door Lord! I can't believe you invited that burp-noggin."

Princess Bubblegum did *not* invite that burp-noggin, the Door Lord. No one invites Door Lords *anywhere*, because they steal people's junk, and then they just—*poof!*—escape through magic doors. And they don't even talk—they mumble and make weirdo giggling sounds. They're all-around *creeps*.

"Look out, PB!" shouts Finn, as the uninvited Door Lord

vaults over the Candy Corn Hole Booth. He swoops down and—
yoink!—grabs all of the princess's birthday presents, including
the giant chocolate-stuffed banana!

"What the junk!?" Finn yells. "He's stealing the presents!
Those are P-Bubs's!"

Jake is *heated*. "He took the chocolate-stuffed banana! *MY*
chocolate-stuffed banana!!"

"Door Lord, give back my friend's presents!" Finn yells.

Suddenly—

KRAK-A-WHOOSH!!!!

From out of nowhere—an icy blast! Finn turns to see a
silvery-white ice bolt rocket through the air and explode against
the Fudgy Ferris Wheel.

It's the Ice King! He's hurling ice bolts at the Door Lord!

ICE-KA-BOOM!!! The Tic-Tac-Toffee Booth is blown to
pieces.

"Ice King!" Finn shouts. "What the nuts? Chill out! You're
doing more damage than the Door Lord!"

But the Ice King (ironically, considering his name) will
not chill out. "It's okay, dudes, I'm handling this!" he says. He
begins gearing up for a massive ice assault! Small particles of
ice begin to form around his hands, and then—*HEWWWW*—he
tosses an ice grenade. The giant ice grenade detonates against
the side of Princess Bubblegum's castle, showering the festival
in chunks of frozen frosting and subzero syrup. Candy citizens
flee, screaming their little candy heads off.

"Oh no . . . ," Princess Bubblegum whispers. "The Ice
King just blew up my secret science laboratory!"

Fun fact: Princess Bubblegum is super into science and

5

junk. And some of her experiments are *scary*.

"Is that a bad thing?" Marceline asks.

"I have weirdo experiments in there," Princess Bubblegum says. "Experiments that can *never leave the castle*. Experiments like—"

Before PB can finish her sentence, a huge wave of water rushes out of the castle! The water begins to rise up, standing, forming a figure. It's some sort of *massive water monster*, as tall as the castle, made entirely out of water!

"Well, experiments like *that*!" Princess Bubblegum says.

"A Giant Water Dude?!" Finn exclaims.

"Ugh. Worst. Birthday. EVER!" Princess Bubblegum moans.

The Giant Water Dude stomps across the festival. He crushes the Fruit-Loop-de-Loop beneath his feet. He's coming right for the princess!

"PB, watch out!" Finn yanks her out of the way, just as a giant watery foot smashes down with a *SPLASH*!

The Giant Water Dude crashes through the kingdom wall, sending the princess's ice cream tower tumbling and crumbling to the ground.

At that moment, the Door Lord giggles mischievously and throws a key into the air. A new door unfolds—it's all like, *click, clack, clack*—and the Door Lord leaps through.

Finn looks around. So much damage! What a mess!

"There might be a way to fix all of this," Princess Bubblegum says. "An old experiment of mine hidden deep within the castle's dungeon . . ."

Finn's mind is racing: a rampaging Giant Water Dude, a Door Lord on the loose, and a strange experiment hidden deep in the dungeon. Where should he start?!!

WHICH WAY, DUDE?

If you think Finn and Jake should capture the Door Lord and get Princess Bubblegum's presents back (and Jake's chocolate-stuffed banana), TURN TO PAGE 11

If you think Finn and Jake should chase after the rampaging Giant Water Dude before he destroys everything, TURN TO PAGE 15

If you think Finn and Jake should travel deep into the castle's dungeon and find Princess Bubblegum's mysterious experiment, TURN TO PAGE 46

IT'S ALL GRAVY

"Whoa, where are we?" Jake asks.

Finn looks around—it's *all foggy*! Fog everywhere! Finn doesn't have a *clue* where they are. But he doesn't want to look dumb, so he says: "Well, Jake, uh, it looks like we, uh, took a turn toward the northern region of Ooo, where the old country meets the new country, and then . . ."

"Oh, come on, you dummy," Marceline says. "I'll lead the way."

One by one, they follow Marceline into the fog. Soon, the fog clears, revealing—

The most creeptastic graveyard in all of Ooo!

"A graveyard?!" Finn exclaims. "Can't a dude catch a break?"

"Don't be a baby," Marceline says. "Just be careful not to step on any graves—you'll wake the ghosts, and they're way grumpy in the morning."

As she says that, Jake trots over. He has a bone in his mouth! Finn is freaked. "DUDE! Gross! Don't chow on that bone."

"Jake? Where did you get that?" asks Marceline. "Please tell me you did *not* just dig that up."

"Don't fret, my pale friend!" Jake grins. "I brought this bad boy with me. Sometimes I crave a good snack when we're out adventuring."

8

"Good," Marceline says. "Because we need to get out of here without waking any ghosts—or else we'll become *their* snacks! Coolio? Now, let's move!"

★ ★ **You earn 9 ADVENTURE MINUTES.** ★ ★

Help the dudes through the graveyard maze! Try to avoid dead ends—because they truly are DEAD ends. Mwah-ha-ha!

If you make it to the exit, **FLIP TO PAGE 18**

If you come to a dead end, **FLIP TO PAGE 14**

BEDTIME IN THE BAD LANDS

"This place, what is it?" asks BMO, as they all step through the door.

"Looks like we are in the Bad Lands," answers Finn as he takes in the mysterious, unforgiving wasteland, located near the horrible Desert of Doom.

"Seriously? Can't we go somewhere with a little shade?" groans Marceline. She slips on a pair of long gloves and pops open a supersize beach umbrella.

"Sorry, Princess Darkness," Finn says, sarcastically. "Next time we're saving the day, I'll make sure we only go to Marceline-approved lands."

"What's your damage, dude?" Marceline barks at Finn. "I was just saying . . ."

The gang is exhausted, and it's starting to show.

"Maybe we can rest a minute?" asks BMO.

"Actually, I could use a break to rest my buns," Finn says. "How about you, Jake?"

Jake doesn't answer—he's already curled up in Marceline's lap, fast asleep. BMO crawls up onto Jake's belly, and soon all three of them are slumbering away.

Finn makes his way over to the gang, and snuggles up. "G'night, my buddies."

THE END

COME AND KNOCK
ON OUR DOOR . . .

"We have to get PB's stuff back. All those presents . . . my chocolate-stuffed banana . . . my giant chocolate-stuffed banana!" Jake howls.

"Okay, here's the plan," Finn says. "Ice King, you go after the Giant Water Dude. Freeze him or something. P-Bubs, you head into the dungeon and look for your experiment thing. Everyone else—we're getting PB's presents back!"

"And my chocolate-stuffed banana," Jake says.

"Of course, buddy." Finn grins.

"Sweet plan, amigo!" Jake says as he high-fives Finn. "Now, what door are we going through?"

Finn looks around. The Door Lord left a *bunch* of open doors behind . . . Two of the doors seem to be glowing. One is silvery, one is gold.

★ ★ **You earn 14 ADVENTURE MINUTES.** ★ ★

11

HELP FINN DECIDE WHICH DOOR TO GO THROUGH!

Examine the two images. The first image shows what the scene looked like *before* the Door Lord swiped stuff. The second shows what the scene looked like *after*. Can you figure out what's missing?

If you think the Door Lord stole 10 items, **JUMP THROUGH THE GOLD DOOR AND TURN TO PAGE 26**

If you think the Door Lord stole 8 items, **JUMP THROUGH THE SILVER DOOR AND TURN TO PAGE 61**

DEM BONES!

"JINGO! Check out all these bones," Jake shouts as he dives into a massive pile of jawbones and femurs and elbows. "There's, like, a gabillion of 'em."

"This doesn't feel right," Finn says nervously.

"This is causing me fear!" whispers BMO.

Even Marceline, who lives for scary stuff, is a little nervous about the spooky surroundings. "I think we might have taken a wrong turn somewhere . . . and I think these bones are from *other dudes* who took that *same* wrong turn."

Suddenly, there is a tremendous *ROAR*! Some foul creature is out there, in the darkness, watching them. Waiting to devour them. This is going to get ugly . . .

THE END

AFTER THE
GIANT WATER DUDE!

"Okay, friendos, here's the plan," Finn says. "Ice King, you go after the Door Lord."

"Good luck with that," Jake says. "Door Lords are the worst . . ."

"P-Bubs, you head into the dungeon and look for your experiment thing. We'll handle this big watery monster," Finn continues. "Now, which way did he go . . . ?"

"Let's find out," Jake says, then grabs hold of Finn and gets rubbery and stretchy and elasticizes himself up high over the castle walls. "There!" Finn says, pointing. "I can just make out his big watery head disappearing over the horizon!"

"We will never snag that big creature," BMO says softly.

"Sure we will. We just need them big ole legs to move fast," Jake says as he turns into *giant-size Jake*—all big and tall, as high as the castle walls. "Hop on, dudes!"

Finn, Marceline, and BMO climb up onto giant four-legged Jake's back. Jake takes off running, charging across the castle drawbridge and out onto the grassy plains. His huge legs take the field in long strides.

But finding the Giant Water Dude is not as easy as Jake had expected . . .

The gang soon enters the Cotton Candy Forest. Tall cotton

candy trees grow high into the sky. Jake's head bobs alongside them. The joint is *thick* with trees, and it's tough to see anything.

"I think we lost him," Finn says with a frown.

But then, as they exit a thick grove of cotton candy trees, they spy an enormous lake. A rotted wooden sign on a post reads: WELCOME TO YE OLDE MAGIC LAKE.

And they can't believe what they see next—

"Yo, the Giant Water Dude is reclining in the lake, doing the backstroke!" Jake exclaims. "I'm watching a *water monster* tread *water* in *water*. I think my brain is going to explode."

"This monster is evil *and* relaxed," Finn says, slightly impressed.

Jake cranes his big head around to look at Finn, Marceline, and BMO. "Maybe he's *not* evil . . . ?" Jake wonders.

Finn shakes his head. "No, Jake. He's a giant monster, and he stomped all over the festival. He must be stopped."

Finn hops down off Jake and walks to the edge of the lake. "Hey, water jerk. Give yourself up!" Finn shouts.

The Giant Water Dude stops paddling around, then shouts—in a very deep voice—"LEAVE ME ALONE!!!"

"Whoa," Jake whispers. "I did *not* figure that guy could talk."

"No dice, water jerk!" Finn shouts back.

For a long moment, the Giant Water Dude doesn't say anything. Then he leans down and *whispers* to the lake.

"What's that weirdo doing?" Jake asks.

Suddenly, the water begins to *freeze*. In seconds, the entire lake has turned to ice!

"What the what?" Finn says, way confused. "The Giant Water Dude must be in cahoots with the magic lake!"

Jake walks to the edge of the ice lake and presses his toe onto the ice. "Seems solid," Jake says. "Maybe we can just cross it, no problem?"

★ ★ **You earn 6 ADVENTURE MINUTES.** ★ ★

If you think they should try to cross the icy lake,
TURN TO PAGE 35

If you think they should walk around the lake,
TURN TO PAGE 113

THE DOOR
LORD'S DOOR

The door spits them out onto a strange rocky path. Finn looks up and gasps. Towering over them is a *huge* door. The door frame is all stone, covered in deep black carvings, and the twin doors are massive and wooden.

"Dudes! We made it! This is the Door Lord's door, for sure!" yells Finn. "Now we just need to figure out how to get in . . ."

Jake, Finn, and BMO begin searching. After a few moments Jake is ready to give up. "I guess I don't *really* need a chocolate-stuffed banana . . . ," he sighs.

"If we can't get inside, PB's birthday will be ruined," Finn says.

Marceline shakes her head. "Oh, calm your butts down. I know how we can get in. Look!" she says, pointing to the top of the door. Strange glowing letters read: ONLY THOSE WITH HEARTS OF LOVE CAN CAUSE THIS GIANT DOOR TO BUDGE.

Marceline whips out her radical ax bass and starts strumming a few notes. "We need to sing a song to the door. But not just *any* song. We need to serenade it with a song from the heart—"

"Butts," Jake says confidently. "We need to sing a song about butts. Rubbery butts, tooting butts, big butts, little butts. Butts, brothas—it's all about butts."

18

"No, not butts, you butt!" Marceline exclaims. "We need to sing about something meaningful and true."

"Okay. Well . . . how about my true and meaningful love for that chocolate-stuffed banana?" suggests Jake.

"Or what about a song for Princess Bubblegum? You know, for her birthday?" Finn says.

Marceline thinks for a moment, then says, "BMO, give me a beat!"

BMO begins pumping out a jam, and the gang begins to sing . . .

★ ★   **You earn 17 ADVENTURE MINUTES.**   ★ ★

USE THE KEY BELOW TO HELP THE GANG FIGURE OUT WHAT SONG TO SING ON THE NEXT PAGE.

mp = G   fp = !   ♪ = D   ♩ = T   ♩ = B   𝄢 = J   o = '

𝄴 = A   ♩ = V   ♩ = S   ♪♪♪ = Y   ♮♩ = H   ♫ = I

♯♩ = R   ♩ = N   ♫ = E   ♩♩ = K   𝄞 = P

If they should sing about PB's birthday,
TURN TO PAGE 21

If they should sing about Jake's banana,
TURN TO PAGE 115

PB B-DAY
JAM

The gang sings together, in perfect, beautiful harmony:

PB, it's your b-day!

It's your b-day, PB.

I hope it's realer than 3-D.

For your b-day, PB.

'Cause I'm gonna be your birthday friend,

Until the very, very end . . .

Of

Time.

"That song was so spice!" Jake says.

"Shh!" whispers Marceline. "Look! The door! It's opening!!"

There's a thunderous rumble, and the gigantic door begins to move. The gang carefully creeps through . . .

"Look there," Jake whispers. The Door Lord is in the corner of the room, hunched over, surrounded by presents—including the chocolate-stuffed banana. The Door Lord's tiny head raises and he looks at them, eyes wide, startled.

He shuffles out of the darkness and makes mumble sounds while waving his big, long arms all over the place.

"What's he doing?" asks Finn.

Marceline says, "I think he's thanking us for being such good friends to PB. Y'know, coming all this way to get her stuff back."

21

"So let's grab the junk!" Finn says.

The four friends gather up all the stolen goods. But when Jake tries to take the chocolate-stuffed banana, the Door Lord yanks it away.

"What the lump?" Jake says. "He's going to let us take all the stuff—*except for my chocolate-stuffed banana*?!"

The Door Lord grins like a superweirdo.

"Give me the chocolate-stuffed banana!" Jake yells.

The Door Lord shakes his head—*NO.*

"Give me that banana!" Jake yells louder.

The Door Lord shakes his head again—*NO.*

Jake *lunges* at the Door Lord! The Door Lord does a super-athletic backflip, tosses a key, and rolls through the door!

"You're not getting away that easy, Door Lord!" Jake yells as he charges toward the door and *leaps* through. Finn follows his friend, diving after him, just as the door closes.

Jake and Finn land on soft snow. The Ice Kingdom.

DING!

Another door opens . . .

"I'm coming, Door Lord!" Jake says, leaping through the next door, with Finn in tow.

DING! Another door appears! Jake and Finn jump through the door. Another one appears! Jake and Finn jump through!

Doors keep appearing!

Jake and Finn keep jumping!

It goes on—door after door after door, jump after jump after jump—through the Slime Kingdom and the Breakfast Kingdom and the Mystery Mountains and past the River of Junk and beyond the Nightosphere.

At last, Jake and Finn somersault out of one door into the Grasslands. The Tree Fort looms over them. "Whoa, we're back home," Finn says.

But in front of the Tree Fort are *three doors*. And the doors look exactly like BMO!

"BMO doors?" Jake says. "What the lump?"

★ ★ You earn 34 ADVENTURE MINUTES. ★ ★

One of the images of BMO on these pages is slightly different than the others—and that's the *real* BMO door! Can you figure out which one it is?

If you think it's door #1, **TURN TO PAGE 100**

If you think it's door #2, **TURN TO PAGE 25**

If you think it's door #3, **TURN TO PAGE 88**

A DATE
WITH LSP

Jake and Finn tumble through the door and land with a soft *woomph*. Jake peeks around. They're lying on a cloud.

"Where are we?" Finn wonders.

"OH MY GLOB!" a deep but still feminine voice exclaims.

Jake sighs. It's Lumpy Space Princess. They're in Lumpy Space—the *last* place they want to be right now. "Hello, LSP," Jake and Finn say.

"Hey, boys. Let's hang!" LSP says.

Jake shakes his head. "We can't, LSP."

"C'mon, let's do stuff! Want to see a movie? Let's go see a movie," LSP says.

"Hmm. They have popcorn at the movie?" Finn asks.

LSP says, *"Obviously!"*

"I bet they don't have any chocolate-stuffed bananas . . . ," Jake groans.

THE END

INTO THE
COTTON CANDY FOREST

The gang is spit out of the door. They somersault through the air and tumble out onto a yellow field.

"PHEW!" Finn says, looking around. "The door brought us to the Cotton Candy Forest. We know this place like the back of our butts! No Door Lord can hide from us here!"

The four friends walk through the sweet puffy pink trees. Finn says, "Jake, can you use your nose to sniff out the Door Lord?"

Jake smiles and says, "No problem." Jake's nose begins to grow and grow and grow until he is just *one giant nose.* Nose-Jake sniffs around. "Uh-oh," Nose-Jake says. *"AAAAAAAACCCCCCCCHHHHHHHHHOOOOOOOO!"*

Nose-Jake *sneezes* with such force that half the Cotton Candy Forest is blown to the ground. Finn, Marceline, and BMO are buried in a pile of sweet spun sugar!

BMO whispers, "Gesundheit."

"Goosen heights to you, too, BMO," Jake says.

"Guys! Look!" Finn shouts as he climbs out of the pile of sticky cotton candy. Some of Princess Bubblegum's stuff is hidden beneath the sneezed-down trees.

"The Door Lord definitely came this way!" Finn says. "Let's go get him!"

"And my chocolate-stuffed banana!" Jakes adds.

With that, the gang sets off through the maze of cotton candy trees . . .

★ ★ You earn 6 ADVENTURE MINUTES. ★ ★

NAVIGATE THE MAZE TO HELP THE GANG THROUGH THE COTTON CANDY FOREST!

Keep track of all the items you find along the way.

If you found **1–4** items along your path,
TURN TO PAGE 8

If you found **5–7** items along your path,
TURN TO PAGE 18

If you found **8** items along your path,
TURN TO PAGE 10

THE LAIR OF THE LIQUID SWORD

The gang stands in a silvery-white room made all of ice. The chamber is very quiet. It's colder than the rest of the rooms, Finn notices. He can see his breath.

"It's like a cave inside of a cave inside of another cave!" Jake says. "Who *does* that?"

But Finn doesn't respond. He's too busy staring at the object in the center of the room. Floating there, surrounded by some sort of strange magic energy, is a sword, suspended in midair.

But as Finn steps closer, his heart sinks.

"Wait," Finn says. "That's not a liquid sword! It's made of solid ice. What the what?!"

"Ice is just frozen liquid," Marceline points out.

Finn hangs his head. "But I thought the sword was going to be all watery. This is bunk. We need a real *liquidy* liquid sword to beat the Giant Water Dude!"

Jake reaches through the energy wall and grabs the icy handle and—

"*OWWW!*" Jake shrieks. "It's freezing! I can't even touch it."

BMO tugs on Finn's shorts. "I know, BMO, I see it," Finn says. "But it's not the right sword."

"Gaze closer!" BMO says, pointing to the icy floor. "It is a mystery poem."

Finn drops to his knees. BMO's right! There are tiny words written on the ice beneath the sword. It says:

Only one can grip the sword,
To discover who, count the s-words.
Don't stop searching until you find them all.
Or find yourself in a spiraling fall!

★ ✱ **You earn 25 ADVENTURE MINUTES.** ★ ✱

SEARCH THE PUZZLE ON THE OPPOSITE PAGE AND FIND AS MANY S-WORDS AS POSSIBLE.

```
A X M L I E K F J H F M E J Q
Q P N H S L I M E L N G I G S
H C Z D A V C E B S W C L H N
U S J K R M O U K D Z T U Y O
N B P S L Z T J F H P B L C W
X K U W Z X Q M X Q I F S M O
E S B E H F S U G A R V Z P E
F D R E T V D Z S E P J D R X
O C T T B G T X G F K X X G H
T R I V G A D Q Y H X L F B A
X E J V X L R X R M S V D M K
N R K P Q D C F C J N M Q P V
S D T O N S H M X X A G D C S
F Q O V J T L I G B I N Y I J
Q U B I H X D O F M L O Z T F
S F B L T P R S A V U I D K S
U A K N C F Q N K T J W B V N
F N Z P O U X Y D H X P G U A
```

If you find **5** s-words or more, backward, forward, or diagonally, that means Finn is "the one" who can take the sword. **TURN TO PAGE 40**

If you find **4** s-words or fewer, that means Marceline is "the one" who can take the sword.
TURN TO PAGE 59

LIQUID SWORD?!
GENIUS!

"Liquid sword!" Finn exclaims. "That's genius!"

"I've never heard of any liquid sword," Jake says. "Where do we find it?"

Choose Goose giggles, and his head flops around on his rubbery neck, and he says, *"Travel deep into the kingdom made of ice. Knock on the door and be very nice. Ask politely and the Ice King will say . . . Get outta here! Go away!"*

Jake frowns. "Well, that's not very helpful."

"We probably need to sneak into the Ice Kingdom," Finn says. *"Ninja-style!"*

The gang waves good-bye to the weirdo Choose Goose, then wanders for a very long time—past Lady Rainicorn's stable, along the Royal Tart Path, around the edge of the Desert of Doom, and across the Unknown Lands. At last, they come to the edge of the Ice Kingdom.

Finn eyes the towering castle made all of ice, looming high above them. It's basically a giant *mountain* of ice, topped by snow. The main entrance is a set of windows that look like a weird old face.

But the gang isn't using the main entrance; they're taking the rear . . .

"You think the Ice King will be waiting for us?" Jake asks.

"He better not be. He's supposed to be chasing after the Door Lord, remember?" Finn says.

"Yeah, but you know the Ice King. He probably got a whiff of some princess's hair and went off all kidnap-happy."

Finn waves his hand. "He's a pussycat! If we find him, I'll just pummel him with my power fists! *POW! POW! POW!*"

The gang treks through the snow and around the castle until they come to the rear. Jake knocks on the shiny, bright-blue ice castle walls twice: *TONK TONK!*

"Frozen solid," Jake says.

"There has to be *some* sort of secret entrance. This is a magic king's castle! That's how that sort of thing works," Finn says.

Finn can see their reflections in the icy wall. Vampires can't usually see their reflections, and Marceline hasn't seen hers in a *long* time. Hmm . . .

All of a sudden, without warning, a section of the wall *shatters*.

"I think it's a puzzle!" Finn says. "The Ice King *loves* you, Marceline. His magic must have made your reflection visible—so he probably made the secret entrance something only you can solve!"

★ ★ **You earn 16 ADVENTURE MINUTES.** ★ ★

CAN YOU DETERMINE IF ANY OF THE REFLECTIONS ACCURATELY SHOW MARCELINE'S REAL REFLECTION?

If you think one of the shattered images correctly reflects Marceline, **TURN TO PAGE 87**

If you think none of the shattered images correctly reflect Marceline, **TURN TO PAGE 111**

CROSSING YE OLDE MAGIC LAKE

They step out onto the lake—just as the Giant Water Dude steps off and disappears into the trees in the distance.

"We gotta motor!" Finn says.

And they do. The gang is sprinting across the lake, when—
KRUNCH!

Finn looks down. The ice is cracking beneath his feet! "Uh-oh," Finn says.

"Whoa, look!" Jake says, staring at his reflection in the cracking ice. "I'm handsome down there!"

Finn squints. "That's def weird, because usually you are *not* handsome. Stuff is *different* down there. Our reflections aren't really us!"

"Why?" Marceline wonders.

Finn thinks for a moment, and then says, "This is a magic lake, right? It must be a puzzle! We need to figure out the differences between the real us and our reflections in the ice!"

"Or else what will be happening?" BMO asks.

"Or else this ice keeps cracking, and we start swimming . . ."

★ ★ You earn 8 ADVENTURE MINUTES. ★ ★

35

Help the gang by spotting the differences between their real images and their reflections in the ice. How many differences can you count?

If you think there are three differences,
TURN TO PAGE 60

If you think there are five differences,
TURN TO PAGE 101

CRUSTY STUFF

"Pizza Den?! Dudes, we *need* to go to the Ice King's Pizza Den!" Jake says. "I'm starving!"

They follow the sign to a narrow hallway lined with icy spikes. Soon, they begin to hear a strange sound—a *disgusting* sound. It sounds like hundreds of people coughing up gnarly loogies, all together!

Quietly, the gang steps into a large icy room—and what they see makes their skin crawl! The source of the noise is *beyond* nasty: ice insects—a hundred of them! They're all swarming in the center of the room, crawling over a towering pile of old pizza boxes. Their icy tongues are licking up the old pizza grease!

"*EWWW!!!*" Jake says.

Finn is about to vomit. "I knew the Ice King had that weirdo Ice-o-pede, but this is *disgusting*!" he says.

Marceline holds back her own puke. "Ice King dumps all his old pizza boxes down here? Why is he so nasty?"

"Where does he get pizza delivery from?" Jake wonders. "I wonder if they'll deliver to us . . ."

"Stay quiet," Finn whispers. "Let's just try to tiptoe around this revolting mess."

But as soon as they take another step into the room, two

Ice Toads spot them! Ice Toads are ugly little frogs, made entirely of ice. Two of the things are squatting on either side of the door. Suddenly, in their froggy voices, they begin shouting, "Alarm! Alarm!"

"Shush!" Jake says. "Be quiet, Ice Toads!"

But it's no use: They're shouting louder now. "*ALARM! ALARM! ALARM!*"

The Ice-sects turn away from the pile of old pizza boxes and march toward the crew. Leading the charge is a huge Ice-corpion (that's a scorpion made entirely of ice). The creature has a long stinger made of ice cubes. Behind it is a huge insect with nasty blue wings—an Ice-cicada! And following that is an Ice-a-pillar—a caterpillar made of ice. Lastly, there are dozens of Ice-ants!

"Finn, I am so freaked, my skin is creeping!" BMO says.

With a heavy *THUD*, the large ice door behind them slams shut.

Jake gulps.

They're trapped.

And the Ice-sects are marching toward them.

But Finn has an idea . . .

★ ★ You earn 31 ADVENTURE MINUTES. ★ ★

UNSCRAMBLE THE LETTERS TO FIGURE OUT HOW JAKE CAN HELP THEM ESCAPE THE ARMY OF ICE-SECTS:

OPTION #1:

KEAJ WEASRTE

OPTION #2:

EJAK TERWATS

If you think they should go with Option #1,
TURN TO PAGE 91

If you think they should go with Option #2,
TURN TO PAGE 83

FINN STEALS
THE LIQUID SWORD

Finn holds his breath. He's nervous. He reaches in and wraps his tiny human hand around the icy hilt. And—

Nothing bad happens.

Finn removes the sword, pulling it from the strange icy energy bubble. Everyone holds their breath—waiting for some disaster to go down. But it's all good in the ice hood. No booby traps and no surprise Gunters.

In Finn's hand, the icy handle of the blade begins to *melt*. Water drips through Finn's fingers and down his arm.

"It's me!" Finn says. "Only I can wield the liquid sword."

Finn slices the blade through the air. "Hi-ya!" Finn yells, swinging the sword at Jake.

Jake ducks. "Careful!"

"It's just water, buddy. Don't be a wussified dog," Finn says, swinging the sword back around, slicing into a large block of ice. The watery blade cuts through the block.

"Dude, it's not just water," Jake says. "It's magic! And you almost cut my head off! I need my head for doin' head stuff."

Of the many swords Finn has held and swung and fought with in his short life, this one is easily the wettest. It is not made of any regular liquid—it is true-blue magical. Yet somehow, even though it is dripping wet, it remains in the form of a blade.

Finn is all pumped now. "Time for us to go catch a Giant Water Dude! Let's roll out!"

But before they can leave, a familiar voice bellows out—

"YOU SHOULD NOT HAVE TAKEN THE LIQUID SWORD!"

Uh-oh.

It's the Ice King.

And he is *fuming.*

TURN TO PAGE 68

41

NOT A
FLAME FAN

"You guys are *not* fans of the Fire Kingdom!" the first Flame Guard says. "Get 'em!"

"I guess that was the wrong answer, Jake!" Finn says.

"And I guess we're fighting now!" Jake responds.

The Flame Guard swings his long flame staff at Finn. Finn springs back as the staff whips through the air with a *whoosh*!

"I will put the pain on you!" BMO cries out, and *charges* the Flame Guard. But BMO simply runs into the Flame Guard's leg and bounces off.

"Puny toy," the Flame Guard says. The Flame Guard raises his foot, ready to *crush* tiny BMO.

"NO!" Finn cries out. He draws the liquid sword and *swings*. The watery blade slices the Flame Guard's foot off!

"Whoa . . . ," Finn whispers. "This liquid sword is *awesome*."

"You want some, too, Flame Guard?!" Finn says, extending the blade and holding it to the other guard's chest.

The Flame Guard shakes his head. "No—no—no, I don't!" he screams, then turns and runs away.

"Cool! I guess it pays to be wrong sometimes, huh?" says Finn.

TURN TO PAGE 73

INTO THE
ICE KINGDOM

Finn looks around. "I think we're in some sort of ice basement . . ."

The room is full of icy exercise equipment: an icy treadmill, an icy bike, and an icy weight machine. There's an icy pool table and an icy bar, with icy mugs and icy glasses.

Hanging from the icy ceiling is a wooden sign. On the sign are two arrows: one labeled THIS WAY TO THE CHAMBER OF FROZEN BLADES and another labeled THIS WAY TO THE PIZZA DEN.

"Hmm," Finn says. "I guess we need to pass through one of these rooms."

"Well . . . ," Jake says. "Which way, dude?"

★ ★   You earn 8 ADVENTURE MINUTES.   ★ ★

If you think the gang should pass through the Chamber of Frozen Blades, **TURN TO PAGE 64**

If you think the gang should pass through the Pizza Den, **TURN TO PAGE 37**

43

APPROACHING THE FIRE KINGDOM

Soon they can see the Fire Kingdom in the distance. And it's not looking good . . .

Usually, the Fire Kingdom is full of lava as far as the eye can see, with a maroon sky and seas of flame. But today, a hazy mist hangs over the kingdom. Steam!

"The Giant Water Dude has been here!" Finn realizes. "We need to get into the Fire Palace, *now.*"

They begin marching down one of the long rocky paths that lead to the center of the kingdom. Blocking the way are two Flame Guards.

"Ah, crud," Finn says. "Flame Guards. I hate these dudes."

Flame Guards are supermean looking. They're covered in black armor, with tiny red arms and legs. Spikes of fire jut out of their heads. They have small, hot red eyes. One Flame Guard holds a long staff that burns bright at the end.

The two Flame Guards spot the approaching gang. "Halt!" the first Flame Guard says.

"Who goes there?" the other Flame Guard asks.

"We need to get inside," Finn says. "There's a big monster stomping all over your kingdom."

"No, there's not," the Flame Guard responds.

"Yes, there is! Right there! I can see him!" Finn exclaims, pointing.

The Flame Guards turn and look. "Oh yeah, you're right," one says.

"Geez, you guys are terrible guards . . . ," Jake mutters.

"Hmm. Seems like we should let them pass," the first Flame Guard says.

"Yeah. But first we need to make sure they are legit fans of the Fire Kingdom," the other Flame Guard says.

★ ★ **You earn 27 ADVENTURE MINUTES.** ★ ★

THIS FINN IS ON FIRE!

How many words can you create from the letters in the word FLAME?

If you think the answer is less than 7,
TURN TO PAGE 42

If you think the answer is more than 7,
TURN TO PAGE 73

FLAME

_____   _____

_____   _____

_____   _____

_____

45

DUNGEON'S
CALLING

"Marceline, you go after that Giant Water Dude," Finn says. "Jake, PB, BMO, and I are traveling down into the dungeons to *turn back time!*"

Marceline walks off, muttering, "This is not how I was planning on spending my day, but whatevs . . ."

"Follow me!" Princess Bubblegum says as they dart through the chaotic, crazy carnival.

"Guys! Guys, wait up!" the Ice King hollers.

"Not you, Ice King!" Jake says.

"What? C'mon! We're buds!" the Ice King says.

"This is all your fault!" Jake yells over his shoulder as he weaves through the crowd.

"I was trying to be a cool hero like you guys!" "No, Ice King!" Finn says, like he's talking to a puppy that just tinkled on the carpet. "NO!"

The Ice King hangs his head as he watches Finn, Jake, BMO, and Princess Bubblegum march into the castle and down to Princess Bubblegum's laboratory, with a plan to turn back time . . .

Inside PB's lab, smaller science experiments like the Frozen Bubble Baby, the Candy Bar Kitten, and the Gumball Gecko have escaped. But they're mostly harmless, and PB is actually curious to see how they do outside the laboratory. Guess now is as good a time as any!

PB brushes aside a bunch of microscopes and beakers, revealing something *awesome*—

A hidden passageway!

Finn smiles. "Hidden passageways are *always* cool."

"This door leads into the dungeon," Princess Bubblegum says. "It's very bad down there."

"So, let's go," Finn says impatiently. He's ready to put an end to this mess!

"Well—um—there's one problem . . . ," PB says. Her face is bright pink—even more than usual!

"What is it?" Finn asks.

"I forgot the password!"

★ ★   **You earn 4 ADVENTURE MINUTES.**   ★ ★

THE GANG NEEDS TO GET DOWN INTO THAT DUNGEON.

Princess Bubblegum can only remember one half of the password—the top half! Fill in the bottom half of the password to open the dungeon door.

ΓΠΠΛ ΓΓΙ ΙΛΠΠ

If you think the password is FINNSSWORD,
TURN TO PAGE 54

If you think the password is PBPASSWORD,
TURN TO PAGE 93

47

TO THE LEFT,
TO THE LEFT

The ball continues rolling and racing—right over a massive underground waterfall! The gang tumbles and tumbles through the air, then splashes down into a huge pool of murky water.

Finn looks up just in time to see the booby-trap bubblegum ball hurtle over them and splatter into the opposite dungeon wall. It explodes in a mess of sticky pinkness.

The gang crawls out of the water and onto the nasty dungeon floor.

"Whoa . . ." Finn looks around and notices two large circles on the wall. "What is THAT?!"

"It looks like a circle with some letters in it," PB says. "But what does it mean?"

★ ★ **You earn 19 ADVENTURE MINUTES.** ★ ★

HELP FINN SOLVE THE TWO CIRCULAR WORD PUZZLES!

Begin with the letter in the center, then read the letters either clockwise or counterclockwise to figure out what the two words are. Then read the two words aloud, and choose your fate.

CIRCLE #1:

R I N
U M O
A T

CIRCLE #2:

T A
I U
M
N I R

If you go with the first word, **TURN TO PAGE 79**
If you go with the second word, **TURN TO PAGE 97**

BONE
TOWN!

Suddenly, the skeletons begin to *move*. Life pumps through them! Their bones rattle as they slowly stand. One of the skeletons hisses—and a stream of goo shoots out of its mouth!

Jake exclaims, "Goo Skulls!"

Goo Skulls are bad news. They're like regular skeleton dudes, but their rib cages are full of oozy green goo! Goo Skulls have all sorts of weird kitchen junk attached to their foreheads—forks and knives and spatulas.

Finn swings his sword and *chops* off the head of one charging goo dude. Jake's rubbery hand turns into a fist and he—*BAM!*—punches two skeletons in their bony butts.

More of them rise! The scattered bones stand and assemble and form an army of Goo Skull villains!

Finn chops, swings, slices, and dices his way through the horde.

CHOP! A Goo Skull is split down the middle!

HACK! Finn knocks a Goo Skull's ugly head right off its bony neck.

SLICE! Finn slashes a Goo Skull right across the chest, cutting it in two.

Finn is a freaking *sword-swinging machine*, slicing and dicing until, at last, they are no more. The Goo Skulls have been defeated.

"Phew," Finn says, catching his breath. "That was serious . . ."

The dungeon room responds to Finn's bravery—the giant door rumbles open . . .

TURN TO PAGE 109

51

FALSE
FINN!

"Whoa!" Jake says. "This is blowing my mind right now! It's like a Finn-stravaganza!"

Before they have a chance to find out if the other Finns are friendly or not, the Finns all start going crazy! The fake Finns pounce on the one, single, real Finn.

"Help!" the real Finn cries out, "I'm being attacked—*by me*!"

But it's too late to help . . .

The fake Finns are beating the *fudge* out of real-deal Finn.

THE END

WRONG TURN, JAKE!

KRAK-A-BOOM!

THE END

FINN'S SWORD IS DEF NOT THE PASSWORD

Suddenly, they're all plummeting down through darkness. Pinwheeling, cartwheeling, and doing a bunch of other types of wheeling.

"I don't think that was the password!" PB says.

"Jake! Where are you?" Finn shouts.

As they fall, BMO flashes a light, brightening up the pitch-black shaft.

"Ow!" Jake shrieks as he bangs his noggin against something. "It's a—*slide*!" he realizes.

BANG! BAM! SLAM! KLUNK! They all smack against the slide, and now they're whooshing down into the darkness . . .

TURN TO PAGE 85

GETTIN' WET
AT THE VET

After a long, *long* walk, the gang arrives at Dr. Doctor's Pet Vet, a veterinarian's office at the edge of the Ice Kingdom.

"Okay, Giant Water Dude, you're home!" Finn says, stepping inside.

The Giant Water Dude bends down and squeezes through the door. He looks around, confused. "Where are we?" he asks.

"The vet! We weren't sure which vet was yours, so we brought you to Jake's," Finn says.

Jake grins. "Dr. Doctor is the best, Giant Water Dude! One time I got my nose stuck in my butt, and he got it out, no problemo."

The Giant Water Dude looks at all the animals waiting and begins to cry. "This is not where I belong," he moans. Massive water-monster tears splash to the ground. In moments, the whole waiting room is filled to the brim with tears!

"I guess he goes to a different vet," Jake shouts as he dog-paddles past Finn.

THE END

CHATTING WITH
THE GIANT WATER DUDE

"I just want to go home!" the Giant Water Dude bellows.

"What home? You're just an experiment gone wrong!" Marceline says.

Finn's mind is racing. "This is sad," he realizes. "Don't you see? This whole time, he was just trying to get home. He didn't even want to destroy the Fire Kingdom. It just happened to be in the way. Giant Water Dude, where is your home?" Finn asks.

But the Giant Water Dude is so sad, he can't answer. Flame Princess is getting impatient. "Come on! Tell us!"

Finn, taking a more Finn-friendly approach, tries to get him to reveal the location of his home . . .

★ ★ You earn 51 ADVENTURE MINUTES. ★ ★

ARRANGE THE LETTER PIECES IN THE SPACES TO FIGURE OUT WHAT FINN SHOULD DO NOW.

If you think they should take him to the ocean,
TURN TO PAGE 75

If you think they should take him to the vet,
TURN TO PAGE 55

BACK TO THE
CANDY KINGDOM!

They all tumble out of the door and crash to the ground. Finn looks around—bright colors and candy junk everywhere. He realizes: They're back at PB's b-day party!

The Door Lord throws a new key into the air, but Jake's not letting the jerk escape that easy!

Jake's legs get all extendified, and he *swats* the key out of the air like a basketball. Finn tackles the Door Lord—*OOMPH!*—and they both hit the ground. Finn loses his grip, and the liquid sword skids away.

The Door Lord squirms away from Finn and tosses *another* key into the air. This dude's got keys for days! He squats down and *launches* himself through the opening door.

"Now what?" Jake asks.

Finn is catching his breath . . .

He's not sure *what* to do next!

SHOULD THE GANG CONTINUE WITH THEIR MISSION TO STOP THE GIANT WATER DUDE?

If so, **TURN TO PAGE 71**

Should the gang go after the Door Lord?
If so, **TURN TO PAGE 26**

MARCELINE'S SWORD HAND IS WEAK

"Are you sure?" Marceline asks. "Me?"

Finn shrugs. "That's what the riddle says. At least, I *think* that's what the riddle says . . ."

Very slowly, Marceline reaches in and wraps her fingers around the hilt and pulls the sword free. "It's all good!" Marceline says. "No worries!"

But then there is a great rumbling. The chamber floor begins to fall away, ice cube by ice cube, one by one!

"The floor is giving way!" Finn exclaims.

The ice continues crumbling! "I think we got the riddle wrong!" Marceline yells.

Every single cube of ice drops away—and below them, there is nothing but pitch-black darkness. The next thing Finn knows, they're all falling, tumbling, spinning, spiraling down into the darkness . . .

THE END

BREAKING
THE ICE

There's another *KRACK!* and a giant fracture shoots through the ice! Finn's foot punches through into the cold water below. "It's freezing!" Finn shrieks.

And then, just like that, a ring of ice breaks, sending them all crashing through and splashing down into the freezing water.

Bad bananas! Jake thinks. *This is bad bananas!*

Finn looks around, frantic, trying to think of a way out, when suddenly—*there*! He sees a flash of light in the water. A door! A *watery* door. *The Door Lord!* Finn thinks. *He must have been here.*

Finn tries to tell the rest of the gang, but he can't talk, because he's underwater and only magic dudes can talk underwater. Finn uses his finger to trace the image of a door in the water.

Jake watches Finn trace the door. He gets it! He turns and starts dog-paddling like crazy. Finn grabs hold of BMO, Marceline grabs hold of Finn, and they all swim down toward the underwater door . . .

TURN TO PAGE 18

DOOMED!

"NERDS!" shouts Finn. "We're in the Desert of Doom!"

The Desert of Doom is one of the worst spots in the Land of Ooo—a vast desert wasteland. Giant rock formations dot the horizon, along with rotted old wooden boats—and *who knows* what scary creatures live in those.

"We need to stick together," Finn says. "Keep an eye out for booby traps, and butterflies with laser guns."

Huddled close together, the gang makes their way through the treacherous desert. They are ducking beneath the bones of an ancient whale, when they stumble into a supersticky mess—

"A gigantic spiderweb! Watch out!" Jake shouts, but it's too late.

"What the what?! Double nerds!" shouts Finn.

"Uh, I think you mean triple nerds," whispers Marceline as she points to three nasty, fur-covered spiders crawling their way.

"Nerds, nerds, NERDS!"

Finn, Jake, and Marceline struggle to free themselves from the web. Worst of all, poor BMO is stuck right at the center . . .

★ ★ **You earn 30 ADVENTURE MINUTES.** ★ ★

CAN YOU RESCUE BMO FROM THE CENTER OF THE WEB BEFORE THE TINY ROBOT BECOMES SPIDER SUPPER?

Navigate the maze and save the tiny robot!

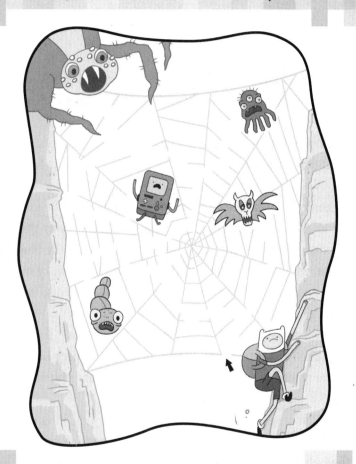

If you reached BMO, **TURN TO PAGE 89**

If you ran into some other nasty creature, **TURN TO PAGE 99**

LIQUID BOARD?
NAH...

"Liquid board?" Finn exclaims. "That doesn't even make sense!"

Jake scratches his head. "Maybe we should've said a liquid fjord?"

"What's a fjord?"

BMO perks up. "Finn, a fjord is a narrow water inlet, surrounded by steep cliffs."

"I don't think any narrow water inlet is going to help us defeat that Giant Water Dude."

"Maybe it's a liquid cord. Like a rope?" Finn says.

Jake shakes his head. "Maybe a liquid award?"

"Why would anyone want a liquid award?!" Marceline exclaims.

"I don't know. To honor their awesomeness?" Jake says.

And it goes on and on like that for hours, with no one ever realizing the one rhyming word they need to stop a liquid villain: *sword*!

Finally Choose Goose quacks and wanders off, muttering to himself, *"Those guys are hopeless—worse than I thought. Now the Giant Water Dude will never be caught!"*

THE END

63

ICE
SICKLES!

"To the Chamber of Frozen Blades!" Finn declares.

The gang passes through a doorway to a winding stairway lined with carvings of strange, spooky ice faces, then they begin marching up.

"I feel like we're going all the way to the top of this freaking pointy ice castle," Finn says. "I'm exhausted!"

"Don't be such a baby, Finn," Marceline says.

"Easy for you to say—you're flying. I've got human legs!"

"Yeah, but flying is tiring," Marceline replies.

"Flying is tiring, flying is tiring," Jake sings.

Marceline groans, then scoops up Finn and carries him like a baby. "How's that?"

"Much better." Finn grins.

After walking up about a million billion icy steps, the gang comes to a doorway. "This must be the Chamber of Frozen Blades!" Finn says.

Hanging from the icy walls are daggers and swords and all sorts of sharp stuff. Lights made of ice dangle from the ceiling. Chunks of strange magic ice float in midair. There are glass cases throughout the room: Inside them are daggers and curved blades and throwing stars.

Finn quickly peers into the cases.

"Argh. I don't see any *liquid* swords!" he says.

Suddenly, there is a sound: "*QUACK!*"

Everyone turns around. It's Gunter! *Many* Gunters. Gunters are the Ice King's penguin pets, and he's got gazillions of them.

"*QUACK QUACK QUACK!*"

"I don't think these Gunters like us sneaking around their daddy's ninja room," Jake whispers to Marceline.

"It's okay, Gunters," Finn says. "We're just looking for something."

"QUACK *QUACK QUACK QUACK QUACK!*"

One of the Gunters waddles over to the wall. "QUACK!" the Gunter says, and presses a button. It feels like the whole castle is shaking! A door opens in the wall, and in charges a horde of Ice Bulls! Ice Bulls are icy villains that look like bulls! They have bright white eyes. Inside their icy bodies are all sorts of visible organs. It's totes weird.

"Ice Bulls!" Marceline exclaims.

"Jake, battle mode!" Finn yells.

An Ice Bull charges! Finn yanks a circular blade from the wall and slashes the rushing beast. The blade cuts into the thing, and the Ice Bull *shatters*! Jake clonks one with a nunchuck, and it bursts into a million pieces. BMO even gets in on the action—whipping throwing stars around the room.

Marceline roars and transforms. Marceline is not your typical run-of-the-mill vampire demon. She's got the power! She can fly, she can disappear, and she can shape-shift into different terrifying things—like a *giant black wolf*. With one bite, she shatters two Ice Bulls with her massive wolf fangs.

Only a single Ice Bull remains . . .

It digs its feet into the icy floor, stirring up a flurry of ice dust. It snorts twice, and then it charges!

"It's time to stop this bull!" Finn says as he leaps to the side and hurls a short sword at the charging ice animal. But the blade misses and flies through a pretty-lady poster hanging on the wall. *RIP!!!* The poster tears open, and the blade keeps going—through the wall!

The Ice Bull is about to spear Finn with one of its big icy horns when Jake yells, "Bull punch!" and leaps in, slamming a big yellow fist into the bull and smashing it.

That's it.

The bulls are defeated.

Finn catches his breath, but just for a moment—

"Look!" Marceline says. "There's a tiny hidden window behind that poster you ripped open!"

The gang runs over. Finn sticks his head through the window. "It's like an icy elevator shaft. Going down!" Finn says.

"But we just came from down," Jake moans.

"Well, we better go *back* down!" Finn says, and with that they all *leap* through the window. They tumble through the darkness. Jake grabs hold of Finn and turns into a rubbery flesh parachute, Marceline yanks BMO out of the air, and they all gently float down to the ice below.

TURN TO PAGE 29

BATTLE IN THE LAIR OF THE LIQUID SWORD

"Finn, Jake, Marceline! And BMO! You're trespassing! Not cool, you jerks."

"Sorry, Ice King, we had to," Finn says. "We needed the liquid sword to stop that Giant Water Dude."

Ice King shakes his head. "I cannot let you leave with the sword."

With that, the Ice King summons an ice bolt and *launches* it at Finn. Finn whips the liquid sword up, and the Ice King's ice bolt *slams* into the blade. The bolt *splits,* and the two halves crash harmlessly into the wall behind Finn.

"Argh!" the Ice King shouts.

The Ice King speaks some magic Fridjitzu words (that's ice-ninja lingo), and an ice sword forms out of thin air! The Ice King shrieks like a lady, then charges Finn, chopping, chopping, chopping with the sword.

Finn slashes. Little droplets of water splash his face as the liquid sword flashes by.

The liquid sword and the Ice King's ice sword meet in midair. It's a collision of H_2O. And the liquid sword is victorious! The Ice King's blade is sliced in half!

"Uh-oh . . ." The Ice King frowns.

He leaps back and blasts ice from his fingertips. Finn leaps into the air as the floor becomes extrafrosty. Marceline yanks Finn out of the air and hurls him toward the Ice King. As Finn flies by, he *swings* the liquid sword. And—*oops*—he slices off the Ice King's—

"Beard! My beard?!" the Ice King shrieks. "Hey! What the junk, Finn?! You chopped off my beard! I need that for doing beard stuff!"

"I had to! Now, I'm sorry, Ice King, but it's time for us to peace out."

"No! I cannot let you leave with the sword! It's mine!"

"Wait a second," Jake says. "You're not even supposed to be here, Ice King! You're supposed to be off chasing the Door Lord!"

The Ice King frowns. "Oops."

"What happened?" Finn asks.

"I got bored. Too many doors," the Ice King says.

Finn shakes his head with frustration.

"Besides, I got that Door Lord good. I stole his hat!" the Ice King says as he reveals a tiny door hat.

Jake shakes his head. "He's going to be mad, Ice King—"

DING!

Suddenly a door appears out of thin air! The Door Lord is back. He flies through the air and into Finn, feet first! *OOOF!* The air goes out of Finn's lungs as he tumbles backward and crashes to the ice. The liquid sword falls from his grip.

"The sword!" Finn yells.

Jake's arm gets rubbery, and he reaches across the room. But it's too late.

The Door Lord grabs the sword, takes back his little hat,

and then, in a flash, tosses a key into the air, and a new door unfolds. He leaps through.

"After him!" Finn shouts.

TURN TO PAGE 58

AFTER HIM!

Finn holds the sword and gives orders. "Ice King, you go after the Door Lord. And don't give up this time! We have to continue chasing the Giant Water Dude."

The Ice King frowns. "Fine," he groans, then leaps through the closing door.

"We have a big problem, buddy," Jake says to Finn. "We don't know where the Giant Water Dude *is*."

"Hmm," Finn says, scratching his head. "If I were a Giant Water Dude, where would I go to do the *most* damage?"

They all think for a moment. Then Jake blurts out, "Duh! The Fire Kingdom!"

Finn's face suddenly gets supersad looking. His eyes are big and watery. "Oh no. Flame Princess . . . ," he whispers. "She's in danger . . ."

Flame Princess is Finn's special lady friend. They've got a serious mushy-mushy love thing going on. If something bad happened to her, Finn would *never* forgive himself!

"We need to get there now!" Finn says.

"Dude, we're way far away," Jake says. "We're all the way back at the Candy Kingdom!"

"Then we'll just have to get there quickly," Finn says. "Let us chart a course, pirate-style!"

★ ✦ **You earn 27 ADVENTURE MINUTES.** ★ ✦

FOLLOW THE MAP TO HELP FINN AND THE GANG GET TO THE FIRE KINGDOM.

START

S two blocks
E one block
SE two blocks
S two blocks

If you land at the Fire Kingdom,
TURN TO PAGE 44

If you land anywhere else,
TURN TO PAGE 120

A FIERY RESCUE

Once inside the kingdom, the crew sees that it's even worse than they had feared. The Giant Water Dude is towering over the castle walls and dealing *major* damage.

But Finn and the gang can't reach him! There are walls of flame *everywhere*. And where there aren't walls of flame, there are huge pools of boiling water.

"We can't pass!" Jake says.

"Oh no," Finn shouts, pointing. "Look. It's Flame Princess!"

Across the kingdom, Finn sees Flame Princess with her flame sword, swinging it at the Giant Water Dude.

"Oh no, he's going to douse her!" Finn says. "We have to do something!"

"I got you!" Marceline says. She scoops up the gang and begins flying . . .

FOLLOW THE MAZE ON THE NEXT PAGE TO RESCUE FLAME PRINCESS!

73

If you land at the Princess, **TURN TO PAGE 102**

If you land at the Water Dude, **TURN TO PAGE 92**

TO THE OCEAN!

"To the ocean!" Finn declares.

But before they can leave, a deep voice hollers out: "HALT!"

It's the Flame King! He marches out of his castle and stands at the edge of a fiery cliff, looking down at the gang. "Do not move," the Flame King says. "Hand over the large water creature who destroyed my kingdom, and you may all go."

"Sorry, Flame King, we can't do that," Finn says. "This water dude is all right. He's just trying to get home and junk."

"Hand him over, or you will all *burn*!" the Flame King roars.

Jake groans. "Ugh, Flame King. More like Lame King, right?"

Flame Princess glares at Jake. "Jake, he's still my dad."

"Right, sorry," Jake says.

Suddenly, an entire *army* of flame demons begin to rise out of the ground. Flame demons are dreadful creatures, made entirely of fire.

"Flame Princess, get home," Finn says. "We'll handle it from here!"

Flame Princess nods. "Be safe, Finn!"

"Come on, Giant Water Dude! We're going to take you home," Finn says—and with that they're sprinting away from the castle, running from an army of flame demons that are— *literally*—hot on their heels.

"I don't like these jerks!" Marceline says, and from out of like, *nowhere*, she whips out her ax bass. Marceline's ax bass used to be a double-sided battle-ax—but now it's a bass guitar. But that doesn't mean the bloodred instrument can't still deal some serious damage.

Marceline slashes a thick mob of the flame demons, and they *explode in a fiery blast*!

"Whoa, Marcy," Jake says. "You can fight fire."

Marceline shrugs. "Y'know. Vampire powers."

Up ahead is a giant cliff. The gang slides to a stop, and Finn peers over the side. Hundreds of feet down is the ocean.

"Home . . . ," the Giant Water Dude says softly, as he stares out at the ocean.

Finn gets a little choked up as he says, "Okay, buddy. I guess this is where we say good-bye."

Marceline sighs. "Can you hurry it up? Remember those guys?" she says, pointing a thumb at the *giant army* of flame demons charging at them.

"Oh, right," Finn says. "Good-bye, Giant Water Dude! I'm sorry I slashed you with my liquid sword."

The Giant Water Dude smiles. "It's okay. I am sorry I got all your stuff wet."

And with that, the Giant Water Dude *leaps* off the cliff. He dives up into the air, flips, does two backward somersaults and three side-spins, then slips gracefully into the ocean.

Jake's impressed. "Whoa. The Giant Water Dude has good form."

"Guys! We'll discuss his diving techniques another time!" Marceline exclaims.

"Let's split!" Finn says, thinking fast. "Um. Um, Jake—hang glider!"

The flame demons are almost on top of them! About to tackle them! Jake transforms into a giant hang glider and shouts, "Grab on!" They do, and Jake *dives* off the cliff. Soon, the entire gang is soaring through the air.

Finn cranes his neck and sees *hundreds* of flame demons running off the edge of the cliff, tumbling over the side and plummeting down into the ocean. "They're not too smart, are they?" Finn notices.

"Yeah, not very *bright*," Jake jokes.

Nobody laughs.

"You know. Bright. Like smart? But also hot?"

Marceline sighs. "I'm flying back home now. I need a break from you lame dudes."

"What do you want to do, BMO?" Finn asks.

"Video games?" BMO asks.

"Radical," Finn says.

And with that, Jake steers left, letting the wind carry them back to the Tree Fort . . .

THE END

JAKE BALL
TO THE RIGHT!

Jake Ball barrels over scattered skeletons, powers through crumbly old doorways, and roars past strange underground trees and metal dungeon gates until, up ahead, Jake sees—

A dead end! A solid brick wall!

"I think we should have gone left, buddy!" Jake says as they race toward the wall. Behind them, the giant ball of bubblegum is closing in! Sadly for our four heroes, it looks like it will be *death by bubblegum*.

THE END

A REAL-DEAL MINOTAUR

From out of the shadows steps a giant, for-real, full-size *minotaur*. It roars—a tremendous, thunderous, gigantic sound.

Jake's ears blow back. "Your breath stinks," Jake says. "You need to floss, brotha."

"Hey, Jake, maybe *don't* insult the giant minotaur," Finn whispers. "Maybe just try to defeat it and get out of here?!"

"But I don't know how to defeat a giant minotaur. Do you?" Jake says. "Hey, um, giant minotaur . . . if one was going to try to defeat a minotaur of your stature, how might they go about that? Where would *you* start?"

The giant minotaur is not amused—its nostrils flare and its hooves dig into the ground. It's getting ready to charge, kicking up crazy dungeon dust! And that crazy dungeon dust causes Jake to start sneezing . . . "*Achooo, achoo, aaaaaccccchoooooooooooo!!*"

Jake pulls out a red hankie to blow his nose, and the minotaur gets a glimpse of it! The minotaur is seeing red! Just as Jake lifts the cloth to his nose, the minotaur *charges*— full speed! Jake, not wanting to spread any nasty Jake germs, politely turns his back to blow his nose. But it's too late for the minotaur to stop! The massively big man-bull powers right past Jake and into the dungeon wall.

KA-BLAM!!!

The minotaur knocks itself out cold!

"DUDE! I think you just defeated the minotaur with your red hankie!" Finn says.

"Sweet! High five!" Jake says, wiping his nose with his hand.

"Aww, gross!"

TURN TO PAGE 109

LET'S GET SCIENCEY!

Finn blinks. The crazy visions are going away. "Phew," Finn says. "Now, PB, where *is* this magic potion thing? We need to *end this*."

Princess Bubblegum agrees. "It's time."

PB walks to the center of the laboratory and yanks away a large white sheet, revealing a complex set of beakers and flasks and graduated cylinders.

"There it is," she says, pointing to the last beaker.

Finn's confused. "In there? That's the Undo-the-Stuffs potion?"

Princess Bubblegum nods and points. "It's that tiny, almost invisible thing. There's just one problem . . ."

Finn crosses his arms. "I was afraid you were going to say that . . ."

"It's very fragile. The chemical reaction—it's unstable . . . If it's not handled properly, it'll explode!" PB warns.

"Well . . . how are we supposed to get it?" Finn wonders.

Jake steps forward and grins. "I think it's time for me to get a little stretchified. And also, a little small. Stretchified and small."

 ★ ★ You earn 48 ADVENTURE MINUTES. ★ ★

81

HELP JAKE NAVIGATE THE MAZE OF BEAKERS, FLASKS, AND SCIENCE JUNK, AND NAB THE UNDO-THE-STUFFS POTION!

If you end up at Potion A,
TURN TO PAGE 53

If you end up at Potion B,
TURN TO PAGE 118

JAKE WITH THE JAKE SWATTER!

"JAKE *SWATTER!*"

Jake raises his arm, and his hand rubberizes and transforms into a big ole yellow *fly swatter* hand!

"Prepare to be flattened, Ice-sects!" Jake yells.

Jake cocks back his swatter hand and then—*whoosh*—he *swats*!

CRACK!

The Jake Swatter hand slams into the Ice-sects! All of them are knocked off their feet and sent soaring through air, into the icy wall, and—*SMASH!*—the army of Ice-sects *explode* into a thousand tiny icy pieces.

"Jake Swatter to the *rescue*," Jake sings.

Finn beams. "Good plan!"

But there's no time for celebrating. The gang crosses the chamber, carefully tiptoeing around the ice remains, and into the next room . . .

TURN TO PAGE 29

BMO
IS THE TRAVELER

"It's BMO!" Finn says. "BMO is the traveler."

The wall is silent for a moment, and then begins changing again. The blocks rearrange back into a mouth, and the mouth says, "YES. BMO IS THE TRAVELER."

The blocks continue to shift and slide, moving and opening to become a doorway. Through the doorway is a very dark winding path.

"BMO, shine us a light," Finn says.

BMO lights up like a flashlight, and they begin walking . . .

TURN TO PAGE 85

SKELETON
DUDES

The gang steps into a hallway filled with skeleton bones—piles and piles and *piles* of dusty white bones.

"There's bad juju down here," Jake says nervously. "I can feel it."

"C'mon," Finn says. "We can't be creeped out. We have to undo everything and fix PB's party."

Just then, Finn's foot catches on something in the ground. "Oof!" Finn yells as he falls. As he looks around, he sees that there are *tons* of old bones in this room. Like, more than a normal amount of bones for a dungeon. Not a good sign . . .

Jake eyes the dungeon door. Etched into the doorway in creepy-looking old letters are the words: COUNT THE BONES TO OPEN THE DOOR. GET IT WRONG, AND THEY RISE FROM THE FLOOR.

★ ✱ You earn 12 ADVENTURE MINUTES. ★ ✱

HOW MANY BONES DO YOU SEE? COUNT THE BONES ON THE NEXT PAGE TO HELP THE GANG ESCAPE!

If you count 16 bones, **TURN TO PAGE 109**
If you count 10 bones, **TURN TO PAGE 50**

MARCELINE'S PRETTY FACE MELTS ICE

"That's it! Good work, Marcy," Finn says.

Part of the icy wall begins to melt, revealing a shiny metal handle. Finn reaches through the melted ice, grabs hold of the handle, and tugs. Suddenly, a door-size chunk of the ice begins to melt away.

"Nice. Door equals found!" Finn says. "I can't believe the only thing in the world that can melt the ice is your pretty face, Marceline. Ice King must have a crush on your face."

"Don't you say that!" Marceline yells. "It's not like that!"

"He totes does." Jake giggles. "*Marceline's face and Ice King sitting in a tree* . . ."

"Ice King is going to proposition a marriage to *your face*," BMO says, joining in on the fun in that cute little BMO voice.

"Let's just get inside," Marceline growls.

Finn, Marceline, BMO, and Jake all step through the secret magic door, into the frozen home of the Ice King . . .

TURN TO PAGE 43

EARL OF
NO-BANANAS-NEVER!

Jake and Finn tumble out of the door and land on a cold stone floor. Jake scratches his head. "Where are we?" he wonders.

Suddenly, a shrill voice shrieks, *"YOUUUU!!!! YOUUUUUU SHOULD NOT BE HERE!"*

Jake knows that voice. It belongs to that nut-bird, the Earl of Lemongrab. He's the yellowy, obnoxious, always-shrieking ruler of the Earldom of Lemongrab.

Jake says, "Sorry, Lemongrab. We're just passing through. Trying to track down a lost banana—"

"NO! NOBODY PASSES THROUGH! NO BANANAS! NEVER! SEIZE THEM!"

"Sorry, buddy," Finn says to Jake as he puts up his fists, ready to knock some heads. "I don't think you're *ever* getting that chocolate-stuffed banana . . ."

THE END

UNStUCk!

Finn draws his sword and starts swinging! The razor-sharp metal slices through stringy webs!

The spider hisses. The vicious, monstrous insect is supremely *ticked off*. It springs forward.

But then—

"GRRRAAWWRRR!!!"

Marceline is shape-shifting into a massive monstrous bat! Bat-Marceline rips free from the webs and swoops down at the spider, hissing and showing off her supersharp, superscary fangs.

The spider shrieks and scurries away, burrowing into the desert sand and disappearing.

Finn finishes cutting up the web, and BMO slips free, dropping to the sand. "I thank you, Ms. Vampire!" BMO says.

Marceline smiles and winks.

"Look!" Finn says, pointing to a shiny reflective glint on the ground. "Two keys! The Door Lord must have dropped them."

Jake snatches them both up and lobs them into the air. *POOF!* Like magic, two doors begin unfolding, one big and one small . . .

If you want to pass through the bigger door,
TURN TO PAGE 18

If you'd rather pass through the smaller door,
TURN TO PAGE 26

JAKE
SWEATER!

"Jake Sweater?!" Jake exclaims. "That doesn't even make any sense!"

Finn scratches his head. "I know. I don't know why I said I that . . ."

"You're the boss, dude," Jake says. With that, Jake transforms into a giant ugly yellow sweater—wrapping around Finn like a gigantic gift from Grandma. Unfortunately, the Ice-sects don't seem particularly impressed by the ugly yellow Jake sweater. The room echoes with icy clicks and clacks as the creepy crawly villains continue marching toward the crew!

Ferocious fanged mouths open and close, and polar pincers pinch!

They're closing in . . .

About to devour the gang . . .

"Whoever thought we should go with Jake Sweater," Finn says, "is a real jerk."

THE END

91

WATER CAN'T DOUSE THE FIRE OF LOVE

"Wrong way!" Jake shouts.

A colossal pool of bubbling lava now separates Finn from the Giant Water Dude and the Flame Princess.

Finn watches in horror as the Giant Water Dude's massive monster hand reaches down and wraps around Flame Princess. She shrieks—a bloodcurdling, water-boiling scream! The water douses her flames! The pained princess collapses to the ground, smoke and steam rising off her body as her skin changes to a pinkish-gray hue.

Finn roars with anger. His love has been hurt. "Argh!" Finn screams as he *races* across the kingdom, his sword raised high in the air, ready to do some chopping.

But *just* before Finn launches his attack, the Giant Water Dude says something that stops Finn in his tracks.

TURN TO PAGE 56

92

PB'S PASSWORD
WAS PERFECT

The door rumbles, then opens, revealing a spiral staircase of stone steps. Spiders creep along the walls. Finn leads the way as candy rats dart underneath his feet.

Jake groans and holds his nose. "It smells like rotten toots down here," he says.

"I haven't been down here in years," Princess Bubblegum says. "All I know is—it's bad."

"What's down here?" Finn asks as he carefully steps through the darkness.

"Failed experiments," Princess Bubblegum says.

"Failed experiments?" Jake asks. "Like what?"

Princess Bubblegum frowns. "Bad stuff. Like the Two-Faced Tooting Tiger Boy, a couple of Nougat Nuggets, and I think there's also a . . . uh . . . a Frosted Finn Butt."

"Not cool, PB," Finn says. "Failed experiments are people, too . . . Wait, a *frosted what what*??!"

"Uh . . . nothing, Finn. Nothing. And these are not people! Trust me!"

"Still. Not cool!" Finn exclaims.

The dungeon is very dark. The floor is cool and made of dirt. The walls are brick. Long brown vines wrap their way around stone corners.

The gang continues their trek through the darkness until they come to a door made of hundreds of small stones. Some of the stones form a mouth. Suddenly, the stone mouth begins moving—the door is *talking*! "One of you who travels holds the key," the door says.

"Huh? What does that mean?" Jake says.

"One of you who travels holds the key. This wall reveals who it be," the talking door says.

"*Who it be?*" Jake repeats, "This door talks like a weirdo pirate."

Suddenly, the stones in the door begin shifting! Some slide up, others slide down, some move left, others move right. They're rearranging!

"I think I got it!" Finn says. "I think I know how we pass."

★ ★ You earn 11 ADVENTURE MINUTES. ★ ★

SHADE IN EACH BLOCK WITH AN X
INSIDE IT TO REVEAL THE
IDENTITY OF THE TRAVELER.

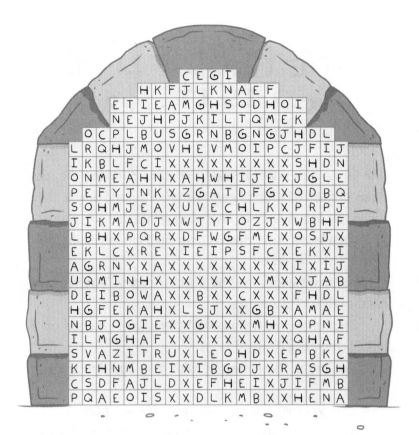

If you think the traveler is BMO,
TURN TO PAGE 84

If you think the traveler is Finn,
TURN TO PAGE 104

THE REAL FINN!
OR IS IT...?

Jake jumps into sidekick mode and starts punching the fake Finns in their fake Finn faces. With just a single punch, they each *explode* into nothing, disappearing into thin air.

When Jake's done, there is only one Finn remaining. Jake beams. "It's you, dude!"

Finn's eyes narrow and he looks very scary. "Are you sure it's the *real* me?" Finn asks.

"OH NO! No, no, no, nooooo!" Jake says. "I messed up. I picked the wrong Finn—"

Finn laughs. "Just messing with you, bud! I'm the real Finn!"

"That was cold, brotha," Jake says. "You scared me!"

PB walks over and places her hand on the door. "Enough joking around, dudes—let's get this over with."

TURN TO PAGE 106

96

MINI-TAURS!

Finn scratches his head. "Wait. *Mini-taur?* I thought the word was *minotaur*. Like a half human, half bull thing?"

Suddenly—*clang, clang, clang, clang, clang!*—a hundred small doors the size of mouse holes open up along the base of the dungeon. Hundreds of small creatures rush out.

"Are those—*mice?*" Jake asks.

Finn says, "They're *tiny minotaurs!* Human bodies with the heads of bulls! They actually are *mini*-taurs!"

And all of a sudden, the mini-taurs are stampeding over everything. A dozen charge at Finn and scamper up his leg. "Get off!" Finn shouts as he unleashes a wicked soccer-style kick, shaking them loose.

"Why don't you play with someone your own size?" BMO says to a charging mini-taur, then whips out a joystick and swings it around like a cowboy trying to rope a bull! Except *this* bull has the legs and upper body of a man! A way tiny, supersmall man, but still . . .

BMO's joystick wraps around the mini-taur. "Gotcha!" BMO says.

But the mini-taur turns and *runs away,* tugging on the joystick wire. BMO tumbles over, and the tiny robot face-plants! "My screen!" BMO shouts.

Jake bends over and *punches* the BMO-harassing mini-taur, sending it cartwheeling through the air.

Suddenly, a rough voice cuts through the darkness. It says, "You touched my babies!"

TURN TO PAGE 79

A Sticky Situation...

"BMO will be spider supper for sure!" cries Marceline.

"And I think we're on the menu, too," Jake moans.

A strand of the spider's web has begun twisting around their legs, and before Finn can grab his sword to free them again, another sticky string is wrapping around his arm!

They're stuck—caught—*trapped!*

"Well, at least I'll be a delish dinner!" Jake says as the web wraps tightly around his belly.

Marceline glares at him. "Really, Jake? That's all you can say at a time like this?"

Jake shrugs. "My guts and stuff taste like sweet vanilla ice cream. I bet you taste like bad cheese and crab goop."

"Your face is crab goop!" Marceline yells.

"Yours is!"

"Is not."

"Is too!"

"IS NOT!"

"IS TOOOOO!!"

The sticky web begins to smother Finn's face. He can't even *wiggle.* And he's stuck listening to Jake and Marceline argue about who's crab goop.

Finn sighs. "I hope these spiders eat me quickly . . ."

THE END

JAKE GOES
BANANAS!

Jake leaps through the door and *tackles* the Door Lord from behind. "Gotcha!" Jake says. "Now give me that banana!"

The Door Lord shakes his head no. This dude won't budge! Jake is mad. Supermad. In fact, Finn's never seen Jake this mad!

And suddenly, Jake begins to transform. His yellow body gets bigger and longer and curvier. Jake is turning into—

A giant banana!

"I AM THE BANANA GOD!" Jake bellows. "HAND OVER THE CHOCOLATE-STUFFED BANANA OR YOU WILL SUFFER THE CONSEQUENCES!"

The Door Lord's eyes go wide, just about popping out of his head. Now the Door Lord isn't going anywhere—he's too *terrified*. He takes a slow step forward and hands the banana to Jake like some sort of offering to the Banana God. Jake yanks it away happily. The Door Lord, just glad to be alive, tosses a key into the air and makes a hurried escape.

Jake says, "Finn, you go now. Follow the Door Lord. Leave."

"Huh? Why?" Finn asks.

Jake gives Finn a weird, sort of *hungry* look. "I want to be alone with the chocolate-stuffed banana."

THE END

ICY
SUCCEss!

The ice stops cracking! It worked! All the cracks uncrack themselves!

"Let's get off this ice sheet now!" Finn says.

Finn, Jake, and BMO slip and slide to the other side of the lake. Marceline hovers above the ice, following them. On the grass, they all happily catch their breath.

Finn looks around for the Giant Water Dude but doesn't see him. "We need to keep walking," Finn says, very determined. Soon, they're once again marching through the Cotton Candy Forest. Finn takes a step and there's a *SPLONK!* sound. Muddy footprints in the grass!

"We must be close!" Finn says.

But the trail of watery footprints does not lead them to the Giant Water Dude. It leads them to someone else entirely . . .

TURN TO PAGE 113

FIRE MAZE
ROCKED!

Finn whips out the liquid sword. The Giant Water Dude is about to reach down and soak the Flame Princess with one of his huge liquid hands.

"NOOOOO!" Finn screams.

Finn leaps through the air and slices off one of the monster's giant watery fingers, just moments before the hand wraps around Flame Princess. The Giant Water Dude howls. His finger splashes against the hot ground, and in moments it's nothing but sizzling steam.

"Thanks, Finn!" Flame Princess giggles and Finn blushes.

"Nice, dude!" Jake says. "You wounded it."

"Oh no—" Finn says.

The Giant Water Dude's finger has rematerialized!

"I create water out of the H_2O in the air," the big water monster dude bellows.

"Oh, crud," Finn moans. "We'll never defeat this dude."

"This is my home! Leave my home!" Flame Princess screams. She unleashes a *fiery fury*. But the Giant Water Dude counters with a blast of water. The two streams—one water, one fire—collide in midair. It's an explosion of white-hot steam! Marceline and Finn and Jake and BMO get back. "It's too hot!"

But the Giant Water Dude is winning. He's pushing Flame

102

Princess's fire blast back. He's too powerful . . .

Marceline realizes she needs to do something.

She darts through the sky, hovering just feet above the white-hot ground, and tackles Flame Princess, pushing her out of the way. The giant blast of water explodes behind her with a *KA-SPLOOSH*!

Flame Princess climbs to her feet. "You're destroying my home! STOP!" she screams.

The Giant Water Dude frowns.

He halts his H_2O assault.

Finn smiles. "Well, that worked. Now what?"

TURN TO PAGE 56

FINN IS NOT THE TRAVELER

"It's me!" Finn says. "Finn the Human!"

The door does not open. Instead, the ground begins to shake. The walls reverberate. Dirt falls from the ceiling. It's like an earthquake!

"Uh-oh, I think that was the wrong answer," Finn says. "And I think the wrong answer triggered some sort of booby trap!"

"Do you guys smell that?" Jake asks. "Smells yummy."

Finn sniffs around. It smells like bubblegum . . .

"Stop sniffing me, Finn!" Princess Bubblegum screams. "It's not me, it's—"

"Ah . . . dudes?" Jake says. "Look—"

Rolling toward them is a *giant* ball of pink bubblegum. It's gargantuan! It's barreling toward them! As it rolls, it picks up chunks of junk from the dungeon floor—bones and rocks and old skeleton guts.

"Oh no. We're trapped like friends in a dungeon," BMO says softly.

"Let's try *this*!" Jake says as he *punches* through the door in front of them, smashing it to pieces.

"RUN!" Finn screams.

They dart through the doorway and down the dark hall.

The booby-trap bubblegum ball is bearing down on them, when—

Princess Bubblegum trips on an old bone in the floor! She stumbles and falls!

"PB!" Finn cries out.

Princess Bubblegum is going to be *crushed* by the barreling ball of bubblegum!

"I got this!" Jake says as he transforms into—

Jake Ball! The greatest ball of all! He's like a giant yellow fleshy bowling ball, just as big as the booby-trap bubblegum ball. Jake rolls over Finn and PB and BMO, sucking them up inside his yellow body.

Jake Ball races through the dark, dank tunnels, rolling end over end. "I'm gonna be sick!" PB says.

Up ahead the tunnel splits. The giant booby-trap bubblegum ball is right behind them!

"Which way, dude?" Jake yells. "There's only two options!"

★ ★ You earn 7 ADVENTURE MINUTES. ★ ★

If you think Jake Ball should roll left,
TURN TO PAGE 48

If you think Jake Ball should roll right,
TURN TO PAGE 78

PB's
LABBY LAB

The door rumbles and opens, revealing a dusty laboratory. "We're here!" Princess Bubblegum exclaims. *"Finally!"*

Finn and Jake look around. The room is stuffed with beakers and test tubes and all sorts of science-type devices. They're all covered in a thick layer of muck, like they haven't been used in forever.

"What is all this stuff?" Finn asks.

"A little of this, a little of that. Over here is what we came for. I call it the Undo-all-the-Stuffs potion. This is totally volatile junk, so be *VERY* careful."

Finn and Jake nod superseriously.

"Y'know . . . ," Princess Bubblegum continues. "Come to think of it, I'm surprised I didn't protect this room with more guards—what with all the horrible things I've created here . . ."

Princess Bubblegum may have spoken too soon. "Did you hear that?" asks Finn as he peers around the lab.

"Did I hear what?" PB asks.

"THAT!" Finn yells as he turns to see an *army* of monstrous creations coming out of the shadows. All of PB's most horrid, evil experiments are revolting against their creator . . .

What was PB thinking, creating all this junk? Finn is

furiously swinging his sword, but he's no match for all these funky evils. He's doomed! They're all doomed.

But then—

There is a tremendous *KRACK* sound and a *BANG* and a great white *flash*, and the monsters are frozen. It's the Ice King! He's saving the day!

"Ice King!" Jake says. "How'd you get here?"

"I just followed you dudes. Thanks for dealing with the skulls and the monsters and the—"

Finn cuts him off. "What the junk, Ice King! What did you do? *I'm, like, blind! Everything looks all jacked up!!*"

Ice King scratches his beard. "Hmm. Maybe I overdid it a little there with the ice flash. Sounds like you've got a case of the Stanky Old Wizard Eyes."

"I can't tell which of these monsters are real and which are just imaginary!" Finn says.

★ ★ You earn 19 ADVENTURE MINUTES. ★ ★

HELP FINN FIGURE OUT WHAT'S REAL AND WHAT ISN'T.

On the next page, the image on the top shows what PB's lab *really* looks like. The image on the bottom shows what Finn is seeing. Count the monsters.

WHICH WAY, DUDE?

If you think there are eight or fewer creatures
that are part of the stanky hallucinations,
TURN TO PAGE 117

If you think there are nine or more monsters
that are part of the stanky hallucinations,
TURN TO PAGE 81

108

MANY, MANY FINNS

"I think we're getting close now!" Princess Bubblegum says as the gang proceeds down the pitch-black tunnel. Rats scurry at their feet.

"It's dark as a butt down here," Jake says. "Are we sure this is the right way?"

"Yep!" Princess Bubblegum says. "There! It's the door to my lab."

A large door looms in front of them. Hanging in front of the door is a strange sort of ceiling lamp shining a bluish-orange light. Finn is running toward the door, when—

"Wait! Finn! Don't step in the light!" Princess Bubblegum shouts. "It's my Multiplier Machine!"

But it's too late . . . Finn walks under the blue-orange light. The ceiling lamp starts shaking and humming and making loud noises like *wah wah wah.*

"What's happening—" Finn starts, but before he can finish his sentence, there is a *flash* of bright light.

When the light finally fades, there are now *six* Finns. And none of them look very happy . . .

★ ★ You earn 6 ADVENTURE MINUTES. ★ ★

HELP JAKE FIGURE OUT WHICH FINN IS THE REAL FINN!

If you think Finn #1, #2, or #3 is the real Finn,
TURN TO PAGE 96

If you think Finn #4, #5, or #6 the real Finn,
TURN TO PAGE 52

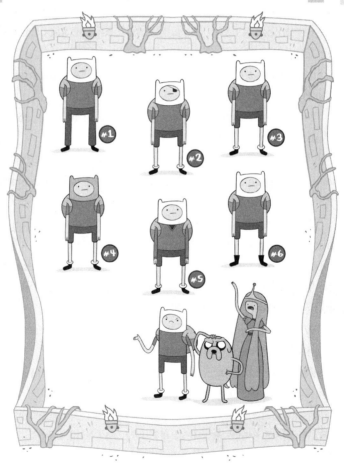

AN iCy
BOOBY TRAP

Marceline steps back and frowns. "I don't get it. My face looks all distorted. I don't think *any* of these reflections are really me . . ."

"Yeah, me neither—" Finn starts to say, but then—

KRUNCH!

A huge crack appears in the castle wall. It starts at the base of the castle and shoots up the side of the wall like a reverse lightning bolt—a line *splitting* the ice.

"I don't think this is good . . ." Jake says.

Small chunks of castle ice begin to break off and fall. One massive piece slides down the side.

Finn's eyes go wide. It's going to hit BMO! "Watch out!"

BMO looks up with wide robot eyes. A huge chunk of blue ice is plummeting down, about to *crush* the tiny robot! In a flash, Marceline darts through the air and scoops up BMO. An instant later, the ice *smashes* against the snowy ground.

"That was a close miss!" BMO exclaims. "Good thing you are a flying vampire hero, Marceline."

Marceline rolls her eyes. "No prob, BMO."

Everybody lies in the snow, catching their breath.

"It was booby-trapped," Finn says. "Ice King booby-trapped his castle!"

Marceline points up to the large hole in the side of the castle.

111

"But, look, we can get in through the hole the booby trap left!"

"NO ICE KING BOOBY TRAPS CAN KEEP US OUT!" Jake shouts. "ONWARD!"

Jake uses his magical legs and stretches high up into the castle opening. Marceline scoops up Finn and BMO and flies up and through the jagged ice hole. Together, they all go down, down, down into the dark depths of Castle de la Ice King.

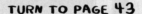

TURN TO PAGE 43

CHOoSE GOOSE
ON THE LOOSE

They step through a large group of trees. A weird, high-pitched voice floats through the air. The voice says, *"Don't know what to do? Let me help you!"*

Finn turns to see the source of the voice: Choose Goose.

"Oh, great," Jake says. He leans close to whisper to Finn, "This guy freaks me out."

That's not a surprise—Choose Goose is a weirdo. He has long orange legs wrapped in striped tights. A big green feather pokes out of his silly blue hat. His eyes point every which way. Weirdest of all, Choose Goose *only* speaks in rhyme.

"Choose Goose! What are you doing here?" Finn asks.

Choose Goose waddles over and says, *"Looks like you have a problem that needs some solving. A water monster that keeps evolving!"*

Finn nods. "Yes. We do."

"How to defeat a villain that's wet? You can figure it out, I bet!" Choose Goose says.

"Just spit it out!" Jake exclaims.

Choose Goose flaps around, then says, *"Come on, genius, use your gourd. To defeat a liquid villain, you need a liquid _ _ _ _ _!"*

 You earn 18 ADVENTURE MINUTES.

113

SOLVE THE PUZZLE TO FIGURE OUT WHAT FINN NEEDS TO DEFEAT THE GIANT WATER DUDE.

There are five *Adventure Time* characters hidden in the word search below. The first letter in each character's name is the clue you need to keep going!

```
T F B R S U W O R M O D X A C G K
K P H M S Q F J E P H R O Q F A J
I A C T C M H K I N I V B T S N G
E J G N O S C D W G D X J C P H O
O S O B R V X B Z S X E Y W L E K
O F F I C E R D A V I S N Q R U C
U B L R H L U F X W C L A X I M A
T K F Q E W T Y E Q M D T H C P R
Y S G B R H V A Z V I O X U A R Z
W D C N J M I L Q J Y H F T R I D
X V Z P T V U D O O R L O R D K M
L I A T O C P K E D O G D F I E N
W U J R V X G N L S R Q B V O W X
```

If you think you need a liquid board,
TURN TO PAGE 63

If you think you need a liquid sword,
TURN TO PAGE 32

114

JAKE'S ODE TO A CHOCOLATE-STUFFED BANANA

Jake belts out a powerful tune from the bottom of his soul:

It's my banana song!

Sing along!

I love you 'cause you're bananas.

Love you more than nails love hammers.

And that is why you are my love . . .

MY BANANAAAAA . . . !

"I can't believe we went with the banana song," Marceline groans.

Jake finishes singing, and everything is silent. Totally zero sounds. They watch the door. Waiting. And then—

KLIK-KLAK-WHOOSH!

The giant door *folds up* and disappears!

It's gone . . .

The song was wrong . . .

"Aw, man! What the junk?!" Jake exclaims. "That song was so boss! The Door Lord wouldn't know a good song if it kicked him in his well-toned butt!"

Finn puts his arm around Jake and says, "I know you loved your chocolate-stuffed banana, but, y'know, if you love something, set it free. Or something . . ."

"I guess you're right," Jake says. "But now what?"

"Let's race back to the fair!" Finn says. "Maybe we can start a *new* plan! We can send the Ice King chasing after that dumb Door Lord—maybe he'll have better luck than us . . ."

TURN TO PAGE 3

STUCK WITH
THE STANK

"Uh-oh, Finn. Looks like you've got the Stanky Old Wizard Eyes worse than I thought. You might be stuck with it . . . ," the Ice King says.

"What?!" Finn cries.

"Listen, it's really not that bad—you get used to it. It's like you're in your own stanky wizard world. You'll see . . . You'll *see*, get it? That part was a joke—the end there . . ."

"Not funny, Ice King," Jake says.

"Too soon?" the Ice King asks.

"TOO SOON!" Jake yells.

Finn, overcome by horrible images, collapses onto the floor and stares at the ground. This whole adventure has been one bad trip—and now it looks like it'll never end!

THE END

GRAND
FINALE!

Jake leaps out of the final beaker and re-biggens himself back to normal size. "Here you go, PB," Jake says proudly. "The Undo-the-Stuffs potion, safe and sound!"

PB yanks a strand of hair from her head, then places a small drop of the potion onto it.

"Here," she says, handing it to Finn. "Chew this."

Finn eyes the strand of hair, unsure. "Really?" he says. "I have to eat your hair?"

PB crosses her arms and nods her head sternly.

"Okay," Finn says. "Here goes."

Finn places the strand of hair onto his tongue, and suddenly everything is happening in reverse. The whole day—it's flashing before Finn's eyes, backward, in superfast-speed mode! It's all like, *VRRRZZOOOORROOOMMMM!*

It's unfolding . . . D-R-A-W-K-C-A-B

And then, just a moment later, the entire gang is back at the party! Everything is the way it was!

And there's the Door Lord leaping through the door. Just like what happened earlier!

Finn says, "Door Lord! Take what you want and go. And Ice King—"

The Ice King says, "Let me guess . . . You don't want me

118

to shoot everything with ice, right?"

"Right," Finn says with a smile.

Princess Bubblegum laughs. "What a day, huh? Best. Birthday. Ever!"

THE END

REVENGE, BEST SERVED COLD

When they finally come to their destination, Finn looks around and exclaims, "OH NO! We're not at the Fire Kingdom—*we're in the Ice Kingdom!*"

Suddenly, Jake shouts, "Watch out!"

"Huh?" Finn says, turning just in time to see—

POW!

A snowball nails Finn right in the kisser and knocks him on his butt. Jake is cracking up. "Gotcha!"

Finn blinks twice, then digs his hand into the snow and pulls out a cold, icy chunk. Finn begins forming it into a ball. He will have his revenge. Oh yes, he will . . .

THE END

WHAT's YOUR ADVENTURE TIME?

Mathematical!

It's time to add up all those Adventure Minutes you earned, and figure out your total super-ultra-awesome **Adventure Time**.

So, how did you do? Did you catch the Door Lord? Did you make things right for the Giant Water Dude? Did you journey deep into the depths of Princess Bubblegum's dungeon and turn back time?

Write your total super top
Adventure Time here!

Want to get an even *bigger* **Adventure Time**? Flip back to page one and start the adventure anew, making different choices!

ANSWERS

PG 9

PGs 12-13

PG 20

PG 34

PG 31

```
A X M L I E K F J H F M E J Q
Q P N H S L I M E L N G I G S
H C Z D A V C E B S W C L H N
U S J K R M O U K D Z T U Y O
N B E S L Z T J F H P B L C W
X K U W Z I B M X Q I F S M O
E S B E H F S U G A R V Z P E
F D R E T V D Z S E P J D R X
O C T T B G T X G F K X X G H
T R I V G A D Q Y H X L F B A
X E J V X L R X R M S V D M K
N R K P Q D C F C J N M Q P V
S D T O N S H M X X A G D C S
F Q O V J T L I G B I N Y I J
Q U B I H X D O F M U O R T F
S F B L T P R S A V U I D K S
U A K N C F Q N K T J W B V N
X N Z P O U X Y D H X P G U A
```

PG 36

PG 47

PBPASSWORD

PG 72

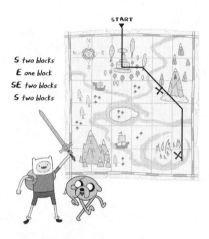

START

S two blocks
E one block
SE two blocks
S two blocks

PG 57

TO THE VAST OCEAN

| TO | TH | E V | AS |
| TO | CE | AN |

PG 74

PG 86

PG 95

BMO

```
              C E G I
      H K F J L K N A E F
    E T I E A M G H S O D H O I
    N E J H P J K I L T Q M E K
  O C P L B U S G R N B G N G J F H D L
L R Q H J M O V H E V M O I P C J F I J
I K B L F C I X X X X X X X X S H D N
O N M E A H N X A H W H I J E X J G L E
P E F Y J N K X Z G A T D F G X O D B Q
S O H M J E A X U V E C H L K X P R P J
J I K M A D J X W J Y T O Z J X W B H F
L B H X P Q R X D F W G F M E X O S J X
E K L C X R E X I E I P S F C X E K X I
A G R N Y X A X X X X X X X X X I X I J
U Q M I N H X X X X X X X X X X M X X J A B
D E I B O W A X X B X C X X X X F H D L
H G F E K A H X L S J X X G B X A M A E
N B J O G I E X X G X X X M H X O P N I
I L M G H A F X X X X X X X X X Q H A F
S V A Z I T R U X L E O H D X E P B X C
K E H N M B E I X I B G D J X R A S G H
C S D F A J L D X E F H E I X J I F M B
P Q A E O I S X X D L K M B X X H E N A
```

PG 108

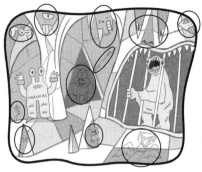

PG 110

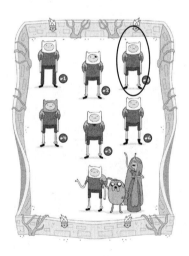

PG 114

SWORD

- Ⓢ SCORCHER
- Ⓦ WORMO
- Ⓞ OFFICER DAVIS
- Ⓡ RICARDIO
- Ⓓ DOOR LORD

```
T F B R S U W O R M O D X A C G K
K P H M S Q F J E P H R O Q F A J
I A C T C M H K I N I V B T S N G
E J G N O S C D W G D X J C P H O
O S O B R V X B Z S X E Y W L E K
O F F I C E R D A V I S N Q R U C
U B L R H L U F X W C L A X I M A
T K F Q E W T Y E Q M D T H C P R
Y S G B R H V A Z V I O X U A R Z
W D C N J M I L Q J Y H F T R I D
X V Z P T V U D O O R L O R D K M
L I A T O C P K E D O G D F I E N
W U J R V X G N L S R Q B V O W X
```